Where is Carl the Corn Snake?

written by Jay Dale

illustrated by Charlie Alder

"Oh, dear!" cried Maya,
looking around the big glass box.
"Where is Carl the corn snake?
I can't see him."

Sam looked in Carl's box, too.
He looked behind some sticks
and leaves.
"He is gone," said Sam.

Carl was the school's pet snake.
All the children loved Carl.

"We have to look for him!"
said Maya.
"He is hiding from us."

The door opened, and in walked
Mrs. Hill with a new teacher.

"Come in," said Mrs. Hill
to the new teacher.
"This is Maya and Sam.
They help to take care
of the school animals."

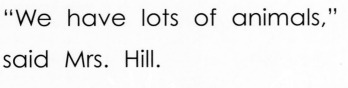

"We have lots of animals,"
said Mrs. Hill.
"We have rabbits and mice,
AND we have a pet snake!"

"Oh, dear!" said the new teacher.
"I don't like snakes at all!"

Bang!

Sam and Maya looked up.

They saw an animal moving

along the bookshelf.

It was long and orange.

It was moving very slowly.

The new teacher looked up, too.

"***Eeeeeeeeekkkkkkk!***" he cried.

"It's a snake!"

He ran out the door

and hid behind a big tree.

Mrs. Hill looked at the children.
Then she looked at Carl.

"Carl got out of his box,"
said Maya.

"We were looking for him."

"But," smiled Sam,

"Carl was hiding from us!"